MathStart™
COUNTING

EVERY BUDDY COUNTS

BY STUART J. MURPHY

ILLUSTRATED BY FIONA DUNBAR

HarperCollins*Publishers*

LEVEL
1

To P.C.T.—whom I know I can always count on
—S.J.M.

To my dear Pano and Helena
—F. D.

The illustrations in this book were done with water soluble crayons on Arches
hot press watercolor paper.

HarperCollins®, 🏭®, and MathStart™ are trademarks of HarperCollins Publishers Inc.

For more information about the MathStart series, please write to
HarperCollins Children's Books, 10 East 53rd Street, New York, NY 10022.

Bugs incorporated in the MathStart series design were painted by Jon Buller.

Every Buddy Counts
Text copyright © 1997 by Stuart J. Murphy
Illustrations copyright © 1997 by Fiona Dunbar
Printed in the U.S.A. All rights reserved.

Library of Congress Cataloging-in-Publication Data
Murphy, Stuart J., date
    Every buddy counts / by Stuart J. Murphy ; illustrated by Fiona
Dunbar.
        p.   cm. — (MathStart)
    "Counting, level 1."
    Summary: A little girl goes through the day counting her "buddies"
which include one hamster, two sisters, three kittens, etc.
    ISBN 0-06-026772-0. — ISBN 0-06-026773-9 (lib. bdg.)
    ISBN 0-06-446708-2 (pbk.)
    [1. Counting.   2. Stories in rhyme.]   I. Dunbar, Fiona, ill.   II. Title.
III. Series.
PZ8.3.M935Ev   1997   95-48840
[E]—dc20   CIP
                                                   AC

1 2 3 4 5 6 7 8 9 10
❖
First Edition

EVERY BUDDY COUNTS

When I wake up feeling lonely—

crummy, yucky, very sad—

I count up all my buddies,

6

and I'm happy, cheery, glad.

I count my little hamster

1 ONE

that I hold in my big hand,

and I count my older sisters

who play trumpets in a band.

2 TWO

I count my cousin's kittens

3 THREE

who always like to play,

and the people in the store

that I visit every day.

4 FOUR

I count my next-door neighbors,

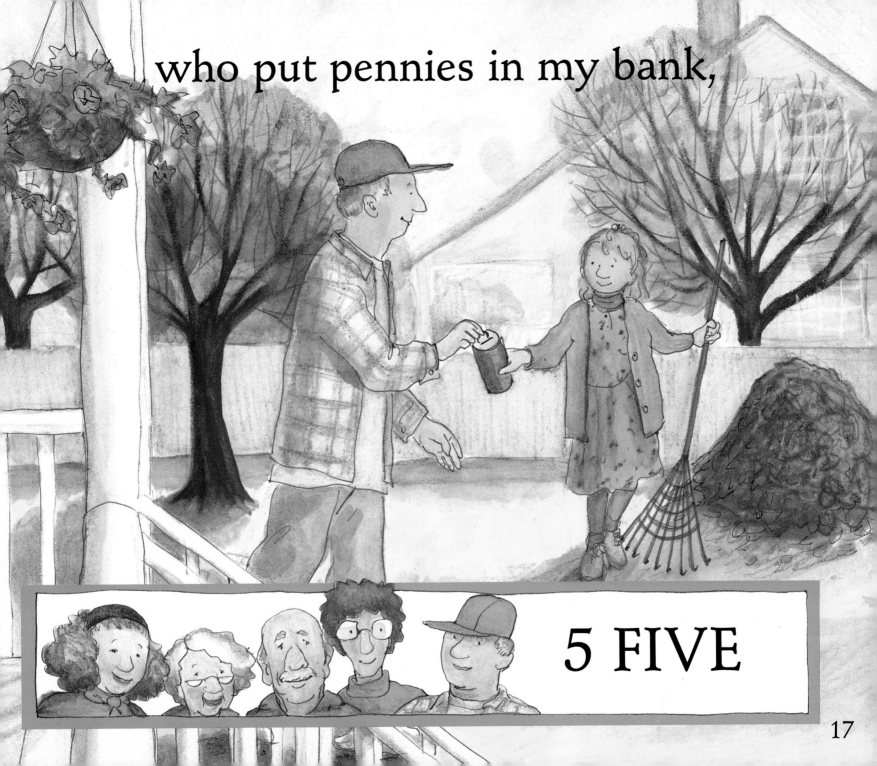

who put pennies in my bank,

5 FIVE

and I count my slinky fish

6 SIX

in their bubbly, bubbly tank.

I count my aunts and uncles

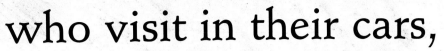
who visit in their cars,

7 SEVEN

and all my favorite playmates

who like to stare at stars.

8 EIGHT

I count my special friends

9 NINE

in the stories I have read,

and my cuddly teddy bears

who snuggle in my bed.

10 TEN

I'm a very lucky person—

as anyone can see.

My buddies can be counted,

1 ONE 	**2 TWO** 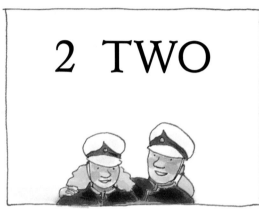	**3 THREE** 
6 SIX 	**7 SEVEN** 	**8 EIGHT** 

and they can always count on ME!

4 FOUR

5 FIVE

9 NINE

10 TEN

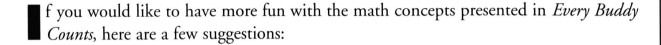

FOR ADULTS AND KIDS

I f you would like to have more fun with the math concepts presented in *Every Buddy Counts*, here are a few suggestions:

- Read the story together and ask the child to describe what is going on in each picture. Point out the numeral and word for each number. Discuss ways in which the girl is being counted on by each of her buddies.

- Ask questions throughout the story, such as "How many older sisters does the girl have?" and "Can you count the number of teddy bears snuggling in her bed?"

- Try counting backward. Open the book near the end and start counting: seven aunts and uncles, six slinky fish, etc.

- Look at the last page of the story. Try counting just the people, or just the animals. Try counting boxes of buddies from top to bottom, or skipping every other box. Can you count how many buddies there are in all?

- Help the child to make his or her own buddy count. Write the names of some of the child's special buddies on note cards. Ask the child to draw pictures of these friends on the cards. Gather the cards in groups: for example, parents, grandparents, play-mates, pets, stuffed animals. Then encourage the child to count the different groups.

- Look at things in the real world and count them. Count the number of buttons on a shirt, toothbrushes in the bathroom, coins on the dresser, plates in the sink, wheels on a bicycle, or toys in a store window.

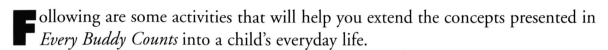

Following are some activities that will help you extend the concepts presented in *Every Buddy Counts* into a child's everyday life.

Cooking: Gather all the things you need to make chocolate chip cookies. How many mixing bowls, measuring cups, and spoons do you have? How many eggs, sticks of butter, cups of sugar or flour are needed? Most important of all—how many cookies did you bake? How many did you eat?

Shopping: As your shopping basket is filled, practice counting what you see. How many jugs of milk or juice are in the cart? How many pieces of fruit? Can you count the number of eggs in a carton?

Taking a Walk: Go for a walk and count the neighborhood sights. How many apartment buildings are on the block? How many houses? Count the number of stores, or the number of windows that face the street. Count trees, streetlights, cracks in the sidewalk, and dogs you see out for a walk, too.

The following books include some of the same concepts that are presented in *Every Buddy Counts*:

• TEN, NINE, EIGHT by Molly Bang

• FISH EYES: *A Book You Can Count On* by Lois Ehlert

• FEAST FOR 10 by Cathryn Falwell